1 The Coda Cer...   ...W6 6AW
...ger.co.uk

First published in Great Britain 2016

Concept by Dana Brown and Maudie Powell-Tuck
Text by Maudie Powell-Tuck
Text copyright © Little Tiger Press 2016
Illustrations copyright © Richard Smythe 2016
Richard Smythe has asserted his right to be identified as the illustrator
of this work under the Copyright, Designs and Patents Act, 1988

A CIP catalogue record for this book is available from the British Library

Printed in China · LTP/1800/1435/0216

2 4 6 8 10 9 7 5 3 1

For Dana, the other half of Team Messy Book
– M P T

For Henry, Darcey and Gertruda
– R S

The MESSY BOOK

Maudie Powell-Tuck • **Richard Smythe**

LITTLE TIGER PRESS
London

I've made a mess.

Maybe you should tidy it up?

Maybe. Or we **could just** . . .

. . . shove it over here!

Ummm. Are we being naughty?

But tidying is *boring*.

We could hide the mess under my bed . . .

or blow it up . . .

. . . or eat it.

wheeeeee!

That is NOT proper tidying.

RUMBLE
RUMBLE
RUMBLE

We've made a mess.